W9-ARC-170

Brothers

Brothers

David McPhail

Houghton Mifflin Harcourt

Boston   New York

MCL FOR
NEPTUNE CITY
PUBLIC LIBRARY

Copyright © 2014 by David McPhail

All rights reserved. For information about permission to reproduce selections from this
book, write to Permissions, Houghton Mifflin Harcourt Publishing Company,
215 Park Avenue South, New York, New York 10003.

www.hmhco.com

The illustrations in this book were done in ink and watercolor.
The text type was set in Calvert MT Std.
The display type was set in Humper.

Library of Congress Cataloging-in-Publication Data
McPhail, David, 1940- author, illustrator. Brothers / David McPhail.
pages cm
Summary: Although two brothers are different in many ways, they are alike, too—
most importantly, in their love for each other.
ISBN 978-0-544-30200-6
[1. Brothers—Fiction. 2. Individuality—Fiction. 3. Love—Fiction.] I. Title.
PZ7.M478818Bqo 2014 [E]—dc23 2013042810

Manufactured in China
SCP 10 9 8 7 6 5 4 3 2 1
4500468806

For my brother Ben—the Dear Boy

This is the story of two brothers.

Most of the time they get along . . .

but not always.

Sometimes they squabble . . .

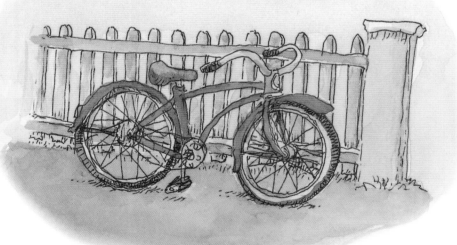

like when they both want to ride the same bike.

So then they take turns.

Sometimes they disagree about whose turn it is to walk the dog . . .

so they walk the dog together.

Brothers can share the blame.

And they take care of each other.
When one hurts his knee . . .

the other pulls him home in the wagon.

Brothers can be both alike and different.

They both like to wear soccer jerseys . . .

but one likes to wear his inside out!

They both like chocolate ice cream.
But one likes his in a cone . . .

while the other insists on a cup and spoon.

One brother can tie his shoes.
The other one . . . not so much.

But he doesn't mind.

Both brothers like to splash in puddles.
One likes to wear his coat, hat, and boots . . .

while the other likes to wear nothing at all!

At bedtime, one brother likes
the window shade up.

The other likes the window shade down.

So they leave it halfway.

If there is thunder in the night . . .

the brothers get under one bed
until the storm passes.

And they know, those brothers do,
that they will stick together . . .

always.